Skeletons

Alan Trussell-Cullen

Australia • Brazil • Japan • Korea • Mexico • Singapore • Spain • United Kingdom • United States

Skeletons

Fast Forward
Blue Level 9

Text: Alan Trussell-Cullen
Illustrations: Gaston Vanzet
Editor: Kate McGough
Design: James Lowe
Series design: James Lowe
Production controller: Emma Hayes
Photo research: Michelle Cottrill
Audio recordings: Juliet Hill, Picture Start
Spoken by: Matthew King and Abbe Holmes
Reprint: Jennifer Foo

Acknowledgements
The author and publisher would like to acknowledge permission to reproduce material from the following sources: Photographs by Ablestock.com, p. 14 right; Istockphoto.com, back cover bottom, back cover top right, pp. 3, 9 bottom, 19 top, 12-13; Lindsay Edwards, p. 8 right; Newsphotos/ Roy Van Der Vegt, p. 11; Newspix/ Mark Graham, p. 7; Photolibrary.com/ IT Stock, back cover top left, pp. 12-13/ Jordan Weinstein, p. 15 bottom/ Knauer/ Johnston, p. 10 bottom/ Michael Fogden, p. 14 left/ Oxford Scientific, p. 9 top right; Photos.com, pp. 4-5.

ISBN 978 0 17 012533 8
ISBN 978 0 17 012525 3 (set)

Cengage Learning Australia
Level 7, 80 Dorcas Street
South Melbourne, Victoria Australia 3205
Phone: 1300 790 853

Cengage Learning New Zealand
Unit 4B Rosedale Office Park
331 Rosedale Road, Albany, North Shore NZ 0632
Phone: 0508 635 766

For learning solutions, visit cengage.com.au

Printed in Australia by Ligare Pty Ltd
8 9 10 11 12 13 14 21 20 19 18 17

Evaluated in independent research by staff from the Department of Language, Literacy and Arts Education at the University of Melbourne.

Alan Trussell-Cullen

Contents

THE SKELETON

The human **skeleton** is made up of all the bones in the body.

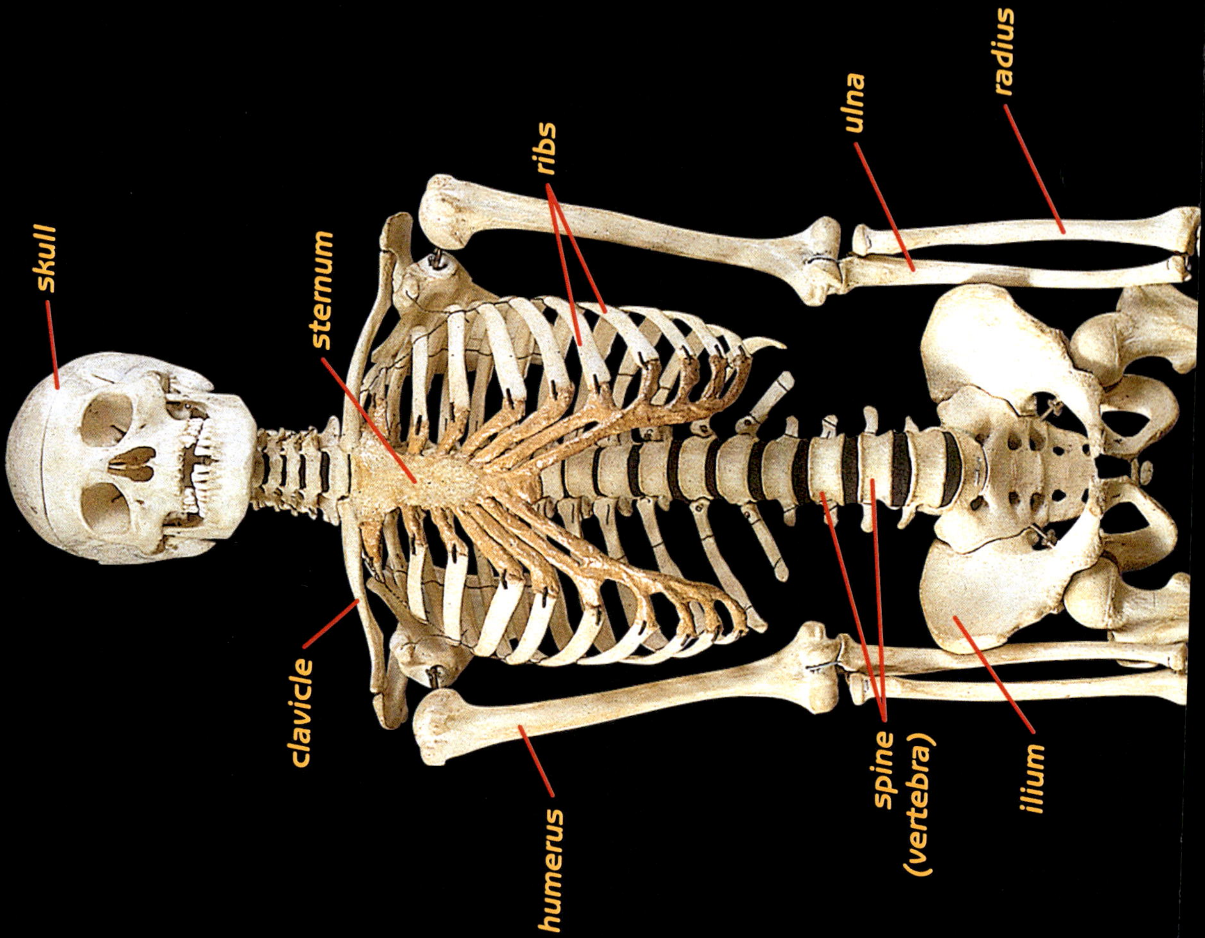

skull
sternum
ribs
ulna
radius
clavicle
humerus
spine (vertebra)
ilium

The skeleton has three important jobs:

- to protect body parts on the inside of the body
- to give the body shape
- to help make the body move.

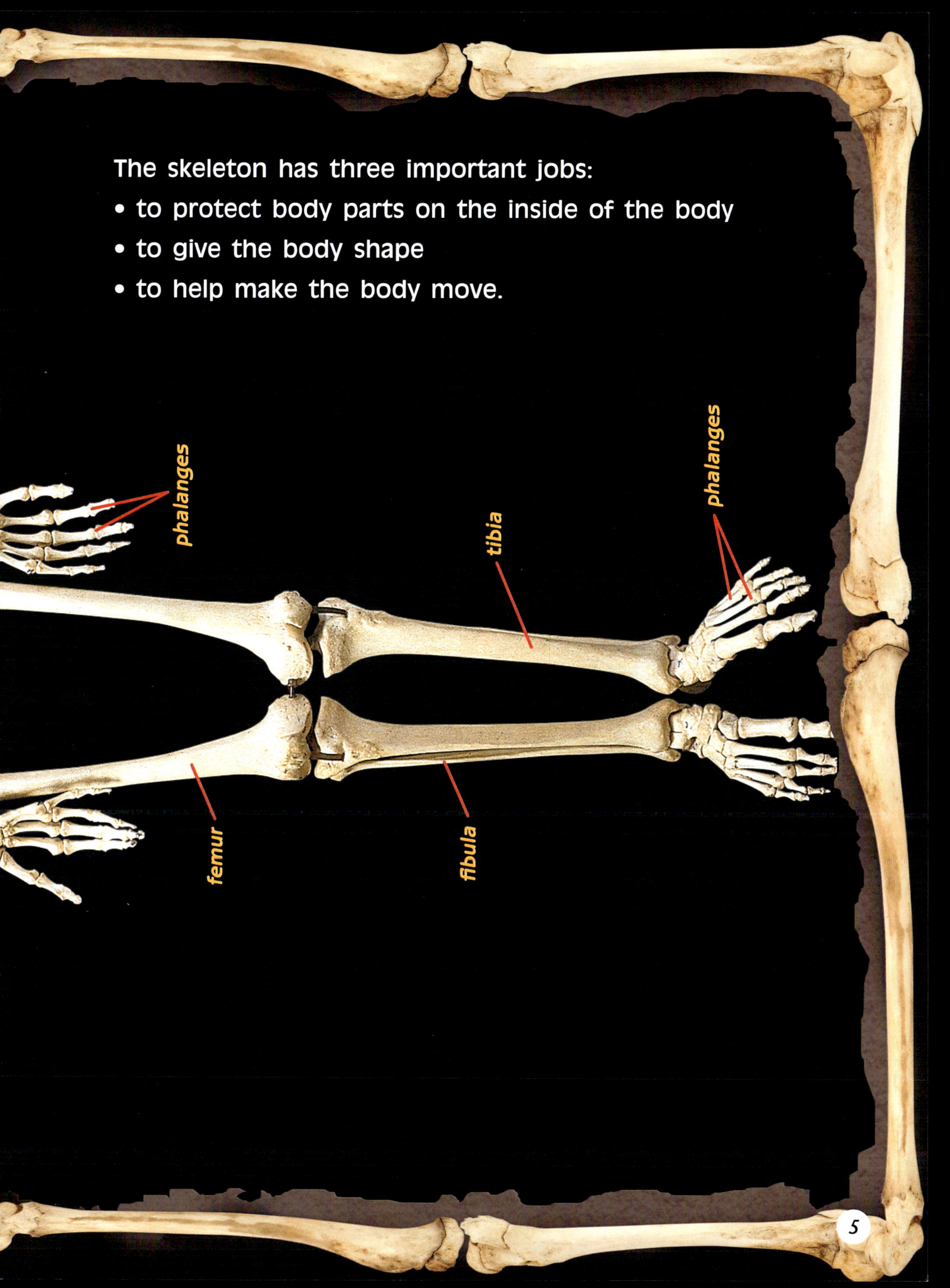

Chapter 2

MUSCLES AND BONES

Bones and muscles work together to make the body move.

Muscles help keep all the bones together. They 'hold onto' the bones in the skeleton.

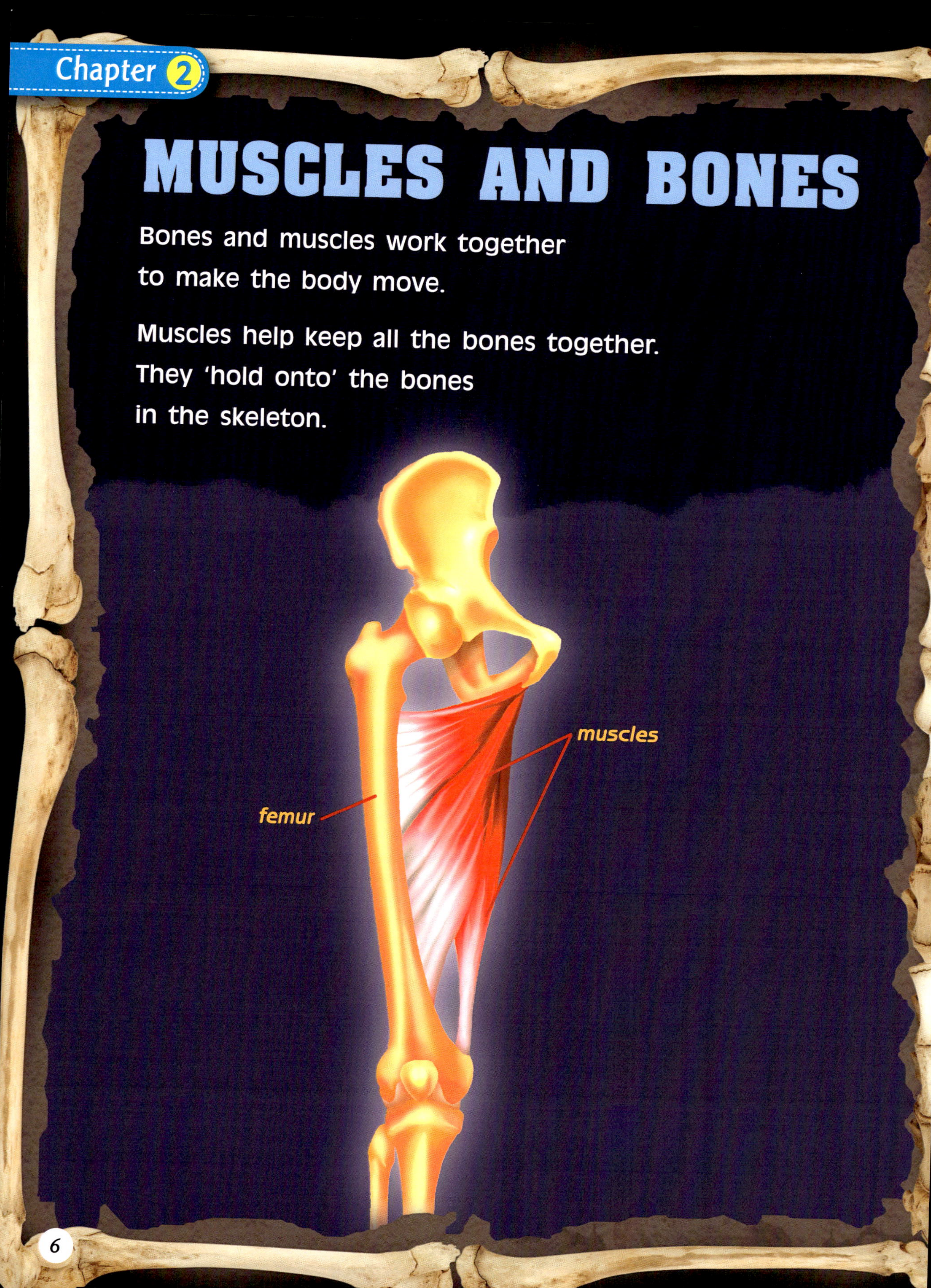

When the muscles move, they move the bones. This makes people move!

Muscle Fact

There are more than 650 muscles in the human body.

Chapter 3

BONES, BONES, BONES!

A human has 206 bones.
A baby starts out with 300 bones, but, over time, some of these bones join together.

Over half of the bones in the body are in the hands and feet.

There are 14 bones in the human face.

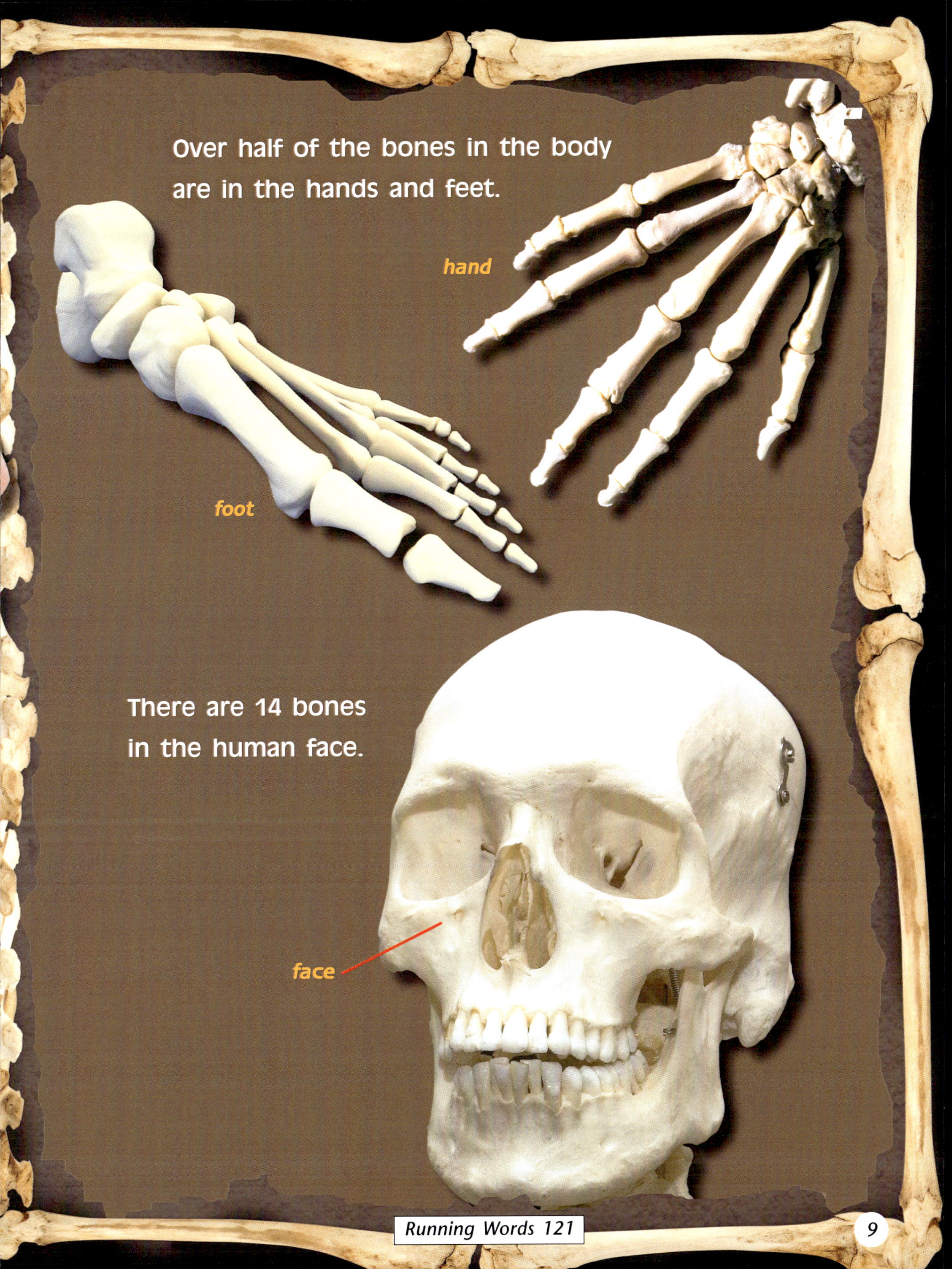

Running Words 121

Chapter 4

STRONG BONES

Sometimes, bones are broken. The good thing is that bones can fix themselves.

It takes about six to eight weeks for a broken bone to mend.

Good food helps bones grow strong and stay strong. These are some foods that are good for bones.

Doing things like running, jumping and playing sports also helps to make bones strong and hard.

Chapter 5

SKELETONS ON THE INSIDE

Like humans, lots of animals have their skeletons on the insides of their bodies.
But not all skeletons are the same.

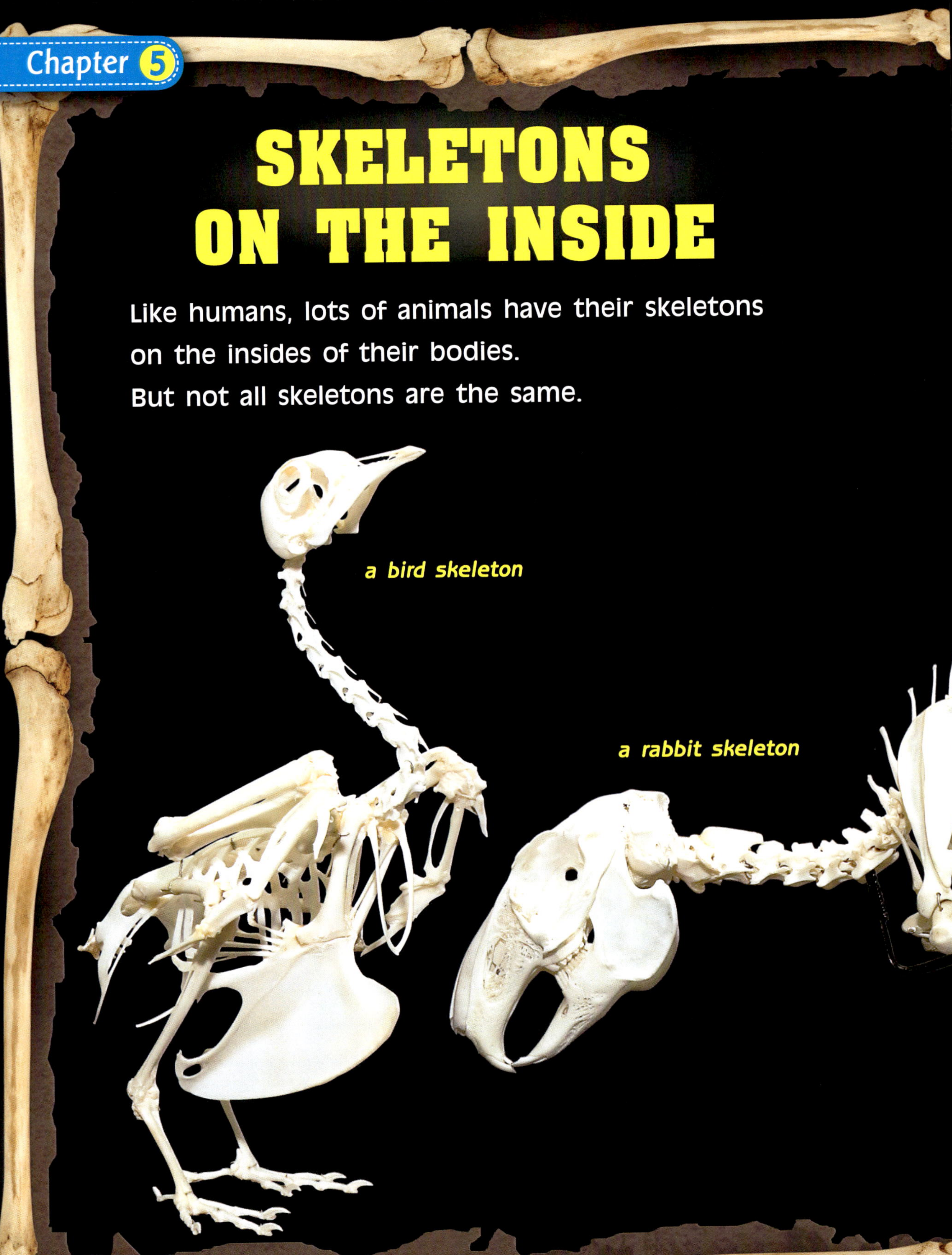

a bird skeleton

a rabbit skeleton

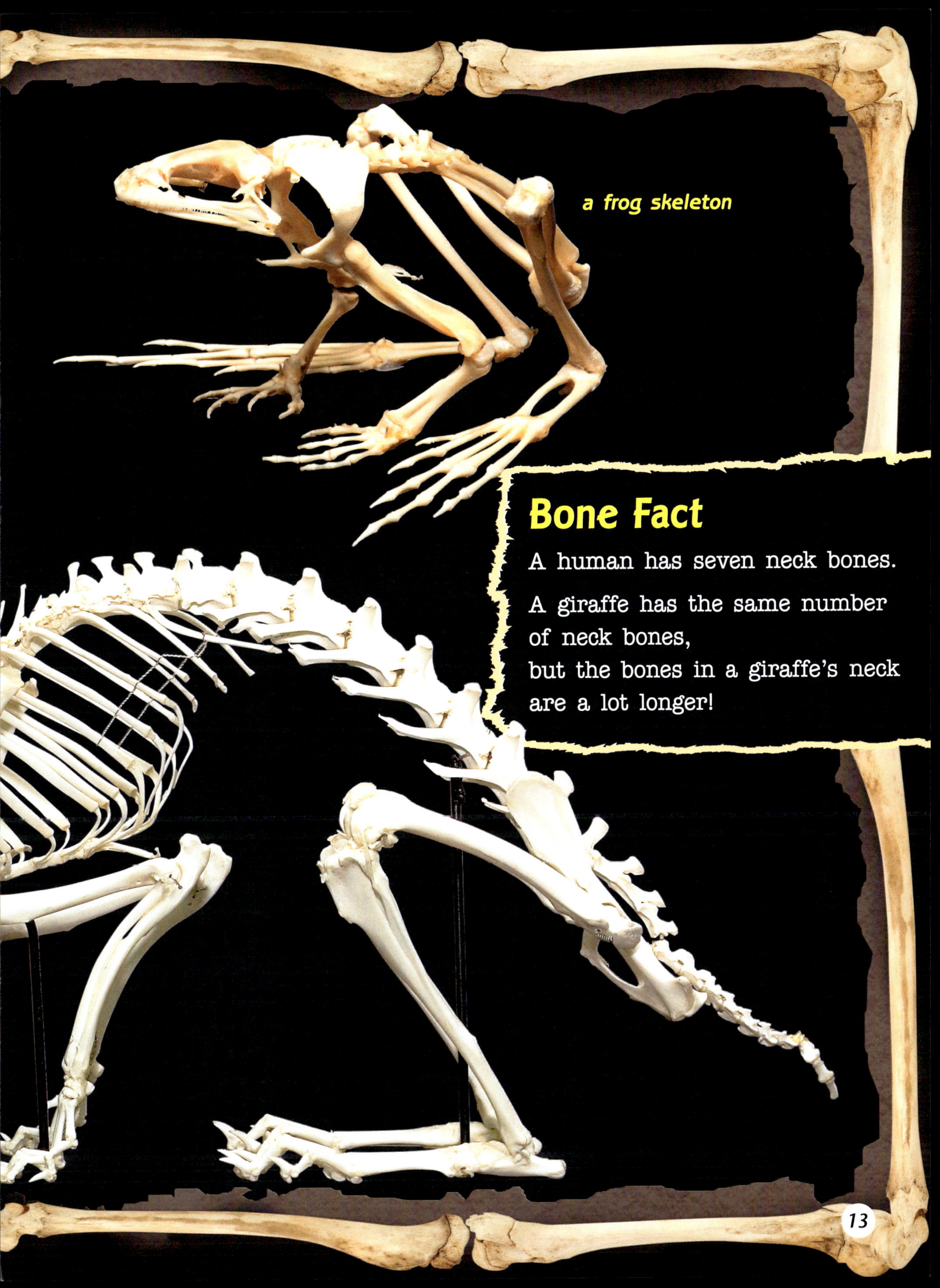

a frog skeleton

Bone Fact

A human has seven neck bones.

A giraffe has the same number of neck bones, but the bones in a giraffe's neck are a lot longer!

SKELETONS ON THE OUTSIDE

Insects have skeletons on the outside of their bodies.

old skeleton

new skeleton

a cicada

When a human grows, the skeleton also grows. But an insect's skeleton does not grow. As the insect grows, it has to grow a new skeleton under its old skeleton. Then it makes its way out of the old skeleton, and leaves it behind.

Coral is an animal that lives in the sea.
It also has its skeleton on the outside.

When you look at a **sea sponge**,
you are really seeing the sea sponge's skeleton.

Glossary

coral a kind of animal that lives in the sea. Coral often looks like it is a plant.

sea sponge an animal that lives in the sea. Like coral, sea sponges often look like plants.

skeleton the hard bones or shell that hold up and protect an animal's body. A skeleton can be inside or outside an animal's body.

Index